Easter

Happy Easter, Finn and Cormac!

We hope you will enjoy this sweet story with such lovely illustrations! We bet you both have dear friends just like Bunny and Bird!

Much love,
Mimi and Doux

Will You Be My Friend?

A Bunny and Bird Story by

NANCY TAFURI

DUCK POND PRESS • CONNECTICUT

Bunny and Bird lived
in an old apple tree.

Bird lived at the top
of the tree
in a little hole.

Bunny lived at the bottom
of the tree
in a big hole.

Bunny wanted to be friends.
When Bird sang,
Bunny came out to listen.
"Will you be my friend?"
Bunny asked.
But Bird felt too shy to answer.
She popped back into
her little hole.

One night,
a big storm came.
The wind blew hard.
Rain fell all around.

Bird hid in her little hole.
Bunny hid in his big hole.

The rain blew
into Bird's home.
She was getting wet.
She started to feel
very, very cold.
Bird did not know where to go
to get out of the storm.
She started to cry.

Bunny heard Bird crying.
He saw that Bird
was getting wet.
"Come down here!"
Bunny called to Bird.

Bird felt shy.
But she was wet.
She was cold.

Bird decided
to take a chance.

She flew
down,
down,
down
to Bunny.

"My home is all wet,"
Bird told Bunny.
Bunny said,
"Come in here
where it is dry."

Bird went in.

Bunny made a cozy bed for Bird.

"Do not worry," he said.

"You are safe here."

Bird felt much better now.
She was warm and dry.

Bunny and Bird fell asleep
on the soft, sweet grass.

The next morning,
Bird's nest was
wet and soggy.
She felt very sad.
"I need a new home,"
Bird said.

Bunny said,
"I am your friend.
I will help you."

Bird flew off
to find soft things
for her new nest.
Bunny set out
to find soft things, too.

Along the way, Bunny met
Chipmunk and Squirrel.

"Will you help fix Bird's home?"
Bunny asked.
"Yes, we will help," they said.

Squirrel found fern leaves
in the woods.

Chipmunk found dandelion fluff
in the meadow.

Bunny found cattail puff
by the pond.

Then they all hurried back
to the old apple tree.

Chipmunk and Squirrel
ran up the apple tree

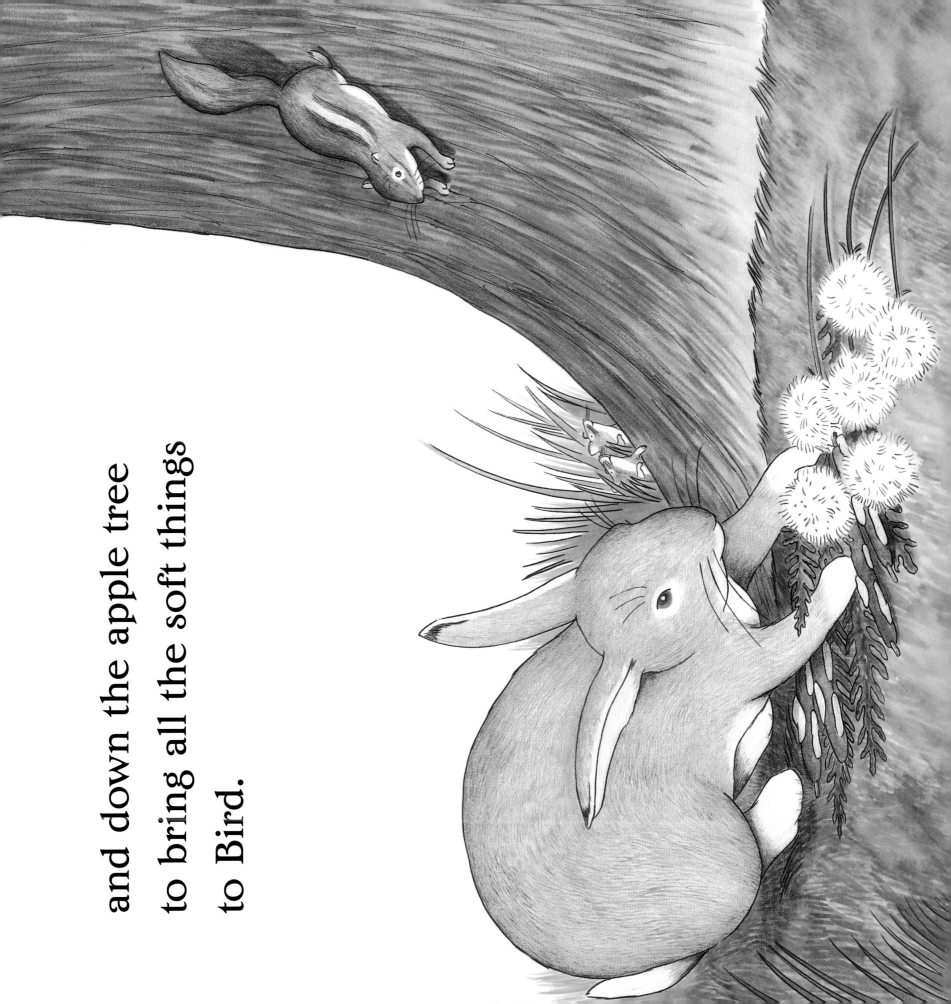

and down the apple tree
to bring all the soft things
to Bird.

Bird tucked the new, soft bedding
into her little hole in the tree.
Soon her new nest was finished.

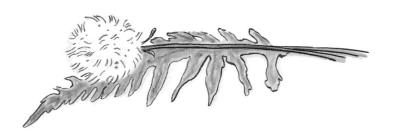

Bird felt warm and happy inside.
She had a new home.
She had new friends.
And she did not feel so shy anymore.

"Thank you," said Bird
to all the animals.
"I never knew I could have
so many friends."

Then Bird flew down
to sing a special song of thanks
for her good friend Bunny.

To Cristina

LIBRARY OF CONGRESS CATALOGING-IN-PUBLICATION DATA

Tafuri, Nancy. Will You Be My Friend ?: a Bunny and Bird story / Nancy Tafuri. - 1st ed. p. cm.

Summary: Bird comes to feel less shy when Bunny helps her rebuild her ruined nest,
showing her what a good friend can be.

ISBN 978-0-9763369-3-8

[1. Rabbits Fiction. 2. Birds Fiction. 3. Friendship Fiction.]

DUCK POND PRESS first edition published in 2013

10 9 8 7 6 5 4 3 2 1

Printed in Malaysia

The illustrations were painted in watercolors and inks.

The text was set in 32 point Edwardian Medium.

Design by Nancy Tafuri and David Saylor